Murder Blooms at the Fair

A Little Firling Mystery – Book Two

by Belinda Chavremootoo

Dedication

For every cat who ever solved a mystery

quietly before the humans caught up.

About the Author

Belinda writes charming cozy mysteries filled with seaside secrets, garden gates, and cats who always know the truth. When not plotting fictional crimes, she can be found in her own garden where the earthy scent of soil and the gentle rustle of leaves provide inspiration. Her two cats supervising everything with quiet judgment.

Table of Contents

Prologue

The first murder came with a sea mist and ended with a pair of muddy boots and a bottle of elderflower cordial. Little Firling had never quite recovered — not from the body, nor from the way retired literature teacher Annabel Lennox Deighton and her slightly psychic cat Persephone unravelled the truth with garden tools, sharp intuition, and an alarming tolerance for nosy questions.

Now, spring has come again. The snowdrops are blooming, the fair is unfurling, and once more, not everything is as sweet as the jam tent.

Chapter 1

It was the kind of spring morning that made everything seem quietly possible.

The sea mist still lingered over Little Firling, softening the hedgerows and the slate roofs, as if the village had been drawn in pencil, then brushed with water. In the back garden of Honeystone Cottage, snowdrops nodded modestly, their white heads drooping like shy guests arriving too early to a party. Nearby, a scatter of hellebores peeked out, blush-toned and slightly dishevelled, thriving in the chilly earth like they'd been here longer than the cottage itself.

Annabel Lennox Deighton knelt beside a patch of rosemary, adjusting its uneven stems with delicate precision. She wore her old gardening jumper — the one with the elbow patches and faint turmeric stains from a Moroccan stew experiment — and a wool headband that Persephone, her sleek Bombay cat, had tried to steal twice already.

Above her, the New Dawn climbing rose had begun its early stretch — burgundy-tipped leaves unfurling like a prelude to a summer symphony that hadn't quite composed itself yet.

"Ambitious," Annabel murmured, eyeing the new shoots. "Especially considering we had a frost last Tuesday."

Persephone, perched high on the garden wall like a feline gargoyle, gave no opinion. Her glossy black fur shimmered in the pale light as she narrowed her golden eyes at a squirrel attempting acrobatics on the bird feeder.

Annabel smiled faintly. "At least someone around here is focused."

She straightened with a soft groan and surveyed her kingdom — a slightly chaotic Eden with dreams of grandeur.

This year, she had plans.

The Desdemona rose — with its peach-blushed petals and a scent like poetry and apricots — would go by the kitchen door. The Double Delight hybrid tea rose, scandalously beautiful with crimson-tipped petals fading to creamy centres, was destined for the gate. And if she could track down a healthy specimen of Madame Hardy, with her pure white blooms and green eye? She'd give it the best spot in the sun.

And the herb patch?

Also due for an upgrade.

She'd been flirting with the idea of Vietnamese coriander, maybe even shiso, if she could convince the local nursery that she wasn't trying to cultivate "exotic weeds." Bronze fennel, lemongrass, perhaps even a few kaffir lime leaves in a pot, just for show. The kinds of things that made her fingers itch to reach for a pestle and mortar.

Her late husband, Michael, used to tease her — *"You collect herbs the way some people collect stamps, darling."*

But he always cleaned his plate.

Those years they spent travelling — narrow street markets in Istanbul, flower carts in Morocco, a guesthouse in Kerala where a woman taught her to make seven kinds of chutney — those flavours still lived in her muscle memory. Her cooking now was a strange fusion of memory and mood.

She wanted her garden to reflect that. More than neat rows. More than polite blooms.

She wanted wildness. Fragrance. Food. Colour. Drama.

Maybe a little too much.

But then again — maybe not enough.

***

By late morning, the village green was in full, unapologetic bloom.

Bunting fluttered overhead, zig-zagging across the stalls like wild ribbon, while the smell of scones, damp grass, and potting soil mixed into something unmistakably English and mildly chaotic.

The Little Firling Annual Garden Fair had drawn a lively crowd — tweed jackets and floral dresses, toddlers with painted faces, labradors in bandanas, and more than one person cradling a prize pumpkin like it was a newborn.

Annabel adjusted the strap of her shoulder bag and surveyed the scene as if preparing for battle.

"Remind me," she said flatly, "how I agreed to be here again?"

Beside her, Evie Barnes, her neighbour and best friend, sipped from a suspiciously floral thermos. "Because you love plants, you're competitive, and deep down, you enjoy village gossip as much as I do."

"That's a lie."

"It's an *accurate* lie."

Persephone, proudly trotting ahead on her red harness (fashionable and deeply resented), paused every few steps to receive praise, attention, and the occasional smoked salmon treat from passersby.

"She's more famous than I am," Annabel muttered.

Evie didn't look up. "She has better cheekbones."

***

The fair spooled out in every direction:

A plant swap stall, where three pensioners were quietly arguing over a mislabelled lupin.

A tea tent with a long queue and a silver urn wheezing like it was doing overtime.

A table full of handmade soaps named things like *'Basil Meditation'* and *'Joy of Geranium.'*

And at the centre of it all, the main stage, where Dr. Alistair Forsyth stood talking with the village council chair and sipping from his familiar porcelain cup.

He looked exactly how a village doctor should — calm, tidy, and vaguely paternal. But something in Annabel's spine prickled.

"Under five minutes," Evie said. "Place your bets on how long before the first scandal."

Annabel opened her mouth to retort —
and the fair delivered.

*****

A shout rose from the competitive
bloom tent.

Florence Cattermole, formidable in
florals, was mid-glare at Ivy Gresham, who
stood coolly behind her herb stall in a linen
wrap dress and earrings that clinked like
windchimes of passive aggression.

"You're selling lies in bottles, Ivy,"
Florence said crisply. "And calling it
medicine."

"And you're selling bitterness in
Tupperware," Ivy replied, "and calling it
chutney."

Several villagers audibly gasped. Someone dropped a bag of potting mix.

"Ladies," said the jam judge nervously, "please. Not in front of the marigolds."

Florence sniffed, shot a look at Persephone — who blinked imperiously — and swept away in a huff that smelled vaguely of verbena.

Evie murmured, "Ivy wins that round."

***

Near the tea tent, Henry Radcliffe, cane in one hand, fury in the other, was gesturing wildly at a sign-up sheet for a "Wellness Walk."

"Oh, he's got the nerve to promote *health*? The man gave me the wrong diagnosis and a ruined spine."

His voice echoed across the fairground, silencing a nearby recorder solo.

Margaret Coombes, trying desperately to stay neutral, put a hand on his arm.

"Henry, not now—"

"When then? After another one of his smug speeches?"

Annabel caught Evie's eye. "Second scandal. That's two in five minutes."

"The villagers are warming up," Evie whispered. "By the time we get to the prize tomato, someone's going to throw a fork."

***

Meanwhile, Colin Denby, wearing his usual field coat and thousand-yard stare, was standing unusually still near the bee display. He bent slightly toward Persephone, who had stationed herself beside a lemon balm plant like she owned it.

"You feel it too, don't you?" he muttered, eyes darting. "Something's off this year. Things growing where they shouldn't. People saying too much."

Persephone licked her paw.

Annabel raised an eyebrow. "Do we think he talks to every cat like that?"

Evie sipped her tea. "Only the sentient ones."

***

Just as the tension reached a polite simmer, the microphone crackled.

Dr. Forsyth took the stage, notes in one hand, teacup in the other.

"Ladies and gentlemen," he said with a smile. "Thank you all for coming to this year's Little Firling Garden Fair..."

Annabel's tea paused halfway to her lips.

Persephone turned to face the stage, tail flicking once.

Evie leaned over. "That's three. Something's coming."

"Under five minutes," Annabel whispered.

Chapter 2

It happened so quickly, at first no one moved.

Dr. Alistair Forsyth was halfway through thanking the volunteers from the Firling Allotment Society when he paused — a faint, odd twitch in his left shoulder. Then he coughed. Twice. A strange, hollow sound that echoed awkwardly over the microphone.

He reached for the lectern.

Then his cup slipped from his hand and fell, shattering on the stage in a porcelain burst that made a woman near the jam tent yelp.

For a breath, it seemed like nothing more than a slip — a simple stumble, a clumsy moment in the middle of a speech no one was particularly listening to.

But then he collapsed, crumpling like a snapped tulip stem.

Flat on his back.

Still.

***

Gasps rolled through the crowd. A child screamed. Someone dropped a tray of meringues.

Evie stiffened beside Annabel. "Bloody hell."

Annabel was already moving. Her instincts — honed from the last murder that had disrupted their quiet lives — prickled like static.

She reached the stage just as Margaret Coombes shoved her way up, her eyes wide and stricken. "Alistair? Oh, God—Alistair?"

But she didn't touch him.

Because even she could see — he was gone.

Annabel crouched, two fingers at the side of the neck, searching for a pulse she knew wouldn't be there. His skin was already cooling. A faint ring of foam clung to the edge of his lip. His eyes, open and clouded, stared at nothing at all.

She gently closed them.

***

Behind her, voices began rising like a kettle nearing boil.

"What's happened?"

"Is it a stroke?"

"Call Dr. Graves!"

"No, he's not here—he's at the racetrack with—"

"Did he eat the chicken salad?! I *told* them not to put that in the sun—"

Annabel tuned them out. Instead, she looked at the small, shattered teacup beside Forsyth's hand. A few drops of tea still shimmered on the stage floor.

Then she felt it.

A gentle nudge.

Persephone had leapt up beside her, sleek and utterly focused, sniffing the air with her ears back.

She gave a low growl — a soft, uncanny sound — then slowly, pointedly, sat beside the broken cup.

***

Evie arrived seconds later, breathless. "Is he—?"

Annabel nodded once.

Evie exhaled through her teeth. "You don't think...?"

"I don't know what I think. Yet."

***

A commotion at the back of the crowd turned every head.

Barrelling toward the stage in a too-large tweed coat and half-laced boots came a man in his early fifties, hair flopping wildly, sunglasses perched like an afterthought atop his head.

He stopped short when he saw the still figure.

"Oh God. Oh *God*."

Graham Forsyth.

Alistair's brother.

And, as rumour had it, his biggest regret.

***

Margaret's voice sliced through the silence. "Where have *you* been?"

Graham looked at her, red-eyed. "I—I didn't know he was—he was *fine*. We spoke yesterday."

"You stink of beer," she snapped. "He asked you not to come today."

"I just—I thought I'd surprise him—"

Evie muttered under her breath, "Well. Mission accomplished."

Annabel glanced between them. The grief looked real... but then again, grief often did.

***

The fair had dissolved into buzzing speculation. A few villagers were crying. Some were shouting. Florence Cattermole was already organizing a crowd control plan near the tea tent. Someone had brought over a gingham blanket to cover the body, but Annabel insisted it stay untouched.

"This is a crime scene now," she said softly.

Graham's head whipped toward her. "What?! What do you mean crime scene? It was a heart attack, right? I mean—Alistair had... had *blood pressure problems,* didn't he?"

Margaret flinched.

Annabel's gaze narrowed. "Did he?"

There was a beat.

Then Margaret said, very quietly, "Not anymore."

***

A few minutes later, Sasha Eldridge appeared at the edge of the crowd, breathless and pale. "Should we call the new doctor? Dr. Graves?"

Evie raised a brow. "Wasn't he invited to the fair?"

Sasha fidgeted. "He said he doesn't really... do events. Likes to keep to himself."

Margaret gave a sharp sniff. "At least he's *consistent.* Unlike Graham."

Annabel turned. "What do you mean?"

Margaret's mouth tightened. "He was meant to be at the races. Alistair told him *specifically* not to come today."

And right on cue, Graham Forsyth barged through the milling crowd — flushed, eyes wide, his coat caught halfway on, and reeking unmistakably of ale and panic.

"What happened?!"

Margaret turned on him like a blade. "Where were you?!"

Graham stammered. "I—I didn't know. He was *fine* yesterday. We spoke!"

"You weren't supposed to be here."

"I came to make things right."

Evie muttered, "Bit late for that."

Before anyone could answer, Persephone let out a low trill — not quite a meow, not quite a growl — as she stared fixedly at Sasha. Sasha backed a step. "What? It wasn't me!"

Persephone blinked slowly. Like she wasn't *convinced.*

***

A few minutes later, PC Tom Oakes showed up — flustered and out of breath, likely pulled off whatever low-stakes bicycle theft had been his only task today.

Margaret explained everything quickly, in a brittle voice.

Tom scratched his head. "So... it might be poison?"

Annabel looked toward the teacup.

"I think," she said, "we need to keep that cup."

"And the thermos," added Evie.

"And *everyone who touched anything near him*," Annabel finished.

Tom sighed. "We'll have to ask some... questions."

Graham let out a strangled sound. "You're not suggesting I had something to do with this—"

"No one's suggesting anything," Annabel said gently. "But Alistair's not going to explain what happened. So, someone else will have to."

***

Later, as the crowd slowly dispersed, Persephone perched on the edge of the stage, watching the last of the fair's banners flutter in the breeze.

A white petal from the rose tent floated past her.

She didn't look away.

Chapter 3

The Hare & Hound smelled of woodsmoke, damp wool, and suspiciously citrusy floor cleaner — all of which Annabel found oddly comforting.

The fireplace crackled. The lamps were lit. And the usual crowd was buzzing like bees that had accidentally found the gin tent.

Evie pushed open the door like a woman on a mission. "Back corner. Less chance of being cornered by Mrs. Pellham and her theories about alien crop circles."

Annabel followed, shrugging off her coat. Persephone padded in ahead of them, tail high, as if she *owned* the pub. Which, to be fair, most of the regulars would agree with.

Henry Griggs, the barkeep, gave her a respectful nod. "Evening, Miss Persephone."

To Annabel: "Sardine pâtés on the house, yeah?"

"Only if she doesn't judge your trousers," Evie said.

Henry grinned. "She already did."

***

They settled into the corner booth, drinks in hand — red wine for Annabel, something mysterious and bubbling for Evie. Persephone curled up regally beside a dish of pâté and a coaster, like a small god waiting for worshippers.

"Right," Evie said, flipping open her notebook. "Where do we begin?"

Annabel glanced around. The pub was already buzzing.

TABLE ONE: Florence Cattermole holding court

"...and I *told* them, didn't I? I said that man was arrogant. Wouldn't even join the WI quiz night. What kind of monster hates trivia?"

Someone murmured agreement.

TABLE TWO: Sasha with suspicious energy

She was hunched over her cider, whispering fiercely to a man Annabel didn't recognize — maybe someone from the pharmacy? Every few minutes she glanced toward the bar like she was expecting someone. Or avoiding them.

TABLE THREE: Colin Denby... muttering

Of course. He had a notepad. A pint. And an audience of one — an uninterested spaniel.

"I said it was coming. Didn't I say it? Everything grows rotten when you bury truth too deep."

The spaniel farted and walked away.

***

Evie leaned in. "Okay, theory time. Top suspect?"

Annabel sipped her wine. "Too soon. But... Margaret was *very* quick to mention Graham had been told to stay away."

"And Sasha looked like someone who'd mixed the wrong file drawer."

Annabel nodded. "And Ivy Gresham? Was she the only one who didn't look surprised?"

***

Just then, the pub door opened — a blast of cold air, and in stepped a man in a charcoal coat and wire-framed glasses.

Dr. Richard Graves.

New GP.

Quiet. Unsmiling.

Like someone who could perform surgery with a teaspoon and not get flustered.

He nodded at Henry, then spotted Annabel.

And *froze.*

Just for a second.

Then he walked to the bar.

Evie said, "You saw that too?"

Annabel murmured, "He wasn't just surprised to see me. He was surprised to be seen at all."

Persephone opened one eye, stared at Graves for three long seconds... and *growled.*

***

Persephone growled — low and definite — as Dr. Graves turned his back to the room.

Evie arched an eyebrow. "Well. That's never a good sign."

Annabel sipped her wine. "She did once growl at a man who stole a wheelbarrow."

"She also growled at a broccoli floret."

Annabel shrugged. "She's discerning."

Just then, a shadow passed their table — and stopped.

Margaret Coombes, still in her nurse's cardigan and a pale green scarf that didn't quite match, stood holding a half-full glass of white wine and an expression that was trying for calm but missing the mark.

"Mind if I join you?" she asked.

Evie opened her mouth.

Annabel beat her to it. "Of course."

Margaret slid into the bench across from them, placing her wine on a coaster with careful precision.

"I suppose you've heard all sorts by now," she said after a moment.

Evie smirked. "Only three murder theories, two poison suggestions, and one claim that Persephone is psychic."

Persephone blinked once. Superior.

Margaret gave a tight, almost-smile. "Alistair wasn't supposed to speak today. He wasn't feeling well."

Annabel leaned in slightly. "What changed?"

Margaret hesitated. "Graham."

Ah.

Evie folded her arms. "I thought he wasn't even invited."

Margaret swirled her wine but didn't drink. "He said he was going to the races. That he didn't want to 'deal with the villagers.' But Alistair was... tense this week. He wouldn't say why. He just said, 'If he shows up, I want the crowd on my side.'"

Annabel tilted her head. "He thought Graham would confront him publicly?"

"I don't know what he thought," Margaret said. "But he cleaned his office. Removed some old files. He was... preparing for something."

Evie frowned. "Or hiding something?"

Margaret's lips pressed into a line.

Annabel was quiet for a long moment. Then: "Did Graham have a reason to want him gone?"

Margaret looked up sharply. "They were *brothers.*"

"Sometimes that's motive enough."

Margaret's hand curled around her glass.

"They didn't speak for over two years. Not properly. Not since the incident with the Radcliffe case. Alistair took the blame. But it wasn't entirely his fault."

Evie's eyes sharpened. "So, Graham *was* involved."

Margaret didn't answer. But her silence was loud.

***

Persephone flicked her tail.

Across the pub, Graham had arrived — slouched into a stool near the window, ordering something cheap and quick. He looked like a man who wanted to disappear into the floorboards.

Margaret stood abruptly.

"I shouldn't have said anything," she murmured. "But I will say this: if Graham *did* come back to make peace... then fate has a cruel sense of humour."

And with that, she slipped away, leaving behind the faint scent of antiseptic and regret.

***

Evie stared into her drink.

"Tell me again why we thought this year would be quieter?"

Annabel sighed. "Because we're optimists."

Persephone let out a long, theatrical sigh.

Annabel nodded. "Exactly."

Chapter 4

The pub had returned to its usual hum — laughter low, pints clinking, conversations humming like bees in thick hedges. But Annabel's gaze never left the man at the far window.

Graham Forsyth, dishevelled and damp around the edges, was hunched over a pint like it might offer absolution. His shoulders sagged in a way that didn't suggest grief exactly — more like exhaustion. Or dread.

Annabel swirled the last of her wine, watching him.

Evie leaned closer. "He's sweating."

"It's warm in here."

"He's sweating like a man who knows the police are going to find something in his sock drawer."

Annabel gave a tiny smile but didn't look away.

***

Persephone, now curled beneath the table, flicked her tail once. A slow, measured warning.

Evie clocked it immediately. "She knows. She *knows* something."

Annabel whispered, "Or she's just bored and wants us to get a move on."

Evie looked toward the bar. "What do we know about him, really? Beyond what Margaret hinted?"

Annabel straightened slightly. "Let's find out."

***

They approached the bar where Henry Griggs was polishing glasses like they'd personally offended him. He glanced up, saw Annabel coming, and raised an eyebrow.

"Let me guess," he said. "You're not here for a refill."

Evie grinned. "We're here for gossip. Just a dash."

Henry huffed, but not unhappily. "Graham Forsyth? Bit of a ghost, that one. Showed up in town a few times over the years. Alistair didn't much like it."

"What did he do?"

"Whatever he felt like. Mostly losing money at the races. Once tried to sell folk on 'vintage jam' made from expired preserves he bought at a car boot sale."

Evie winced. "Yikes."

Henry leaned in. "But here's the weird bit — he came in last week. Dead sober. Asked me if I thought this place was... ready for change."

Annabel's brow furrowed. "Change?"

"That's what he said. Gave me the creeps. Then he tried to tip Persephone with a chip."

From under the bench, Persephone sneezed. Violently.

***

Annabel turned to look back at Graham — just in time to see his chair was empty.

She froze.

"Evie."

Evie spun. "No. No-no-no—he was just *there.* I saw him! You saw him!"

"He's gone."

Annabel scanned the pub. No movement. No back door ajar. Just a faint trace of spilled ale on the floorboards and an abandoned coat on the back of the chair.

Graham Forsyth had vanished.

***

Evie swore under her breath.

Persephone emerged from under the bench like a small panther on a mission and trotted toward the back hallway.

Annabel followed.

"Where does that go?" she asked Henry.

"Rear exit. Leads down by the river path."

Annabel didn't wait.

***

Outside, the air was sharp with mist and something sweeter — early blossom on the hedgerows, maybe. The lights from the pub glowed behind them like a stage curtain.

Ahead: no sign of Graham. Just flattened grass by the gate. Footprints? Hard to say in the gloom.

Persephone paused at the path and sniffed the air.

Then, with perfect confidence, she turned left — into the trees.

Evie hesitated. "Are we actually going to follow a cat?"

Annabel adjusted her scarf. "She's never been wrong yet."

Chapter 5

The mist curled low over the path as Annabel and Evie followed Persephone's determined march through the narrow lane that dipped behind the pub and skirted the edge of the riverbank. The air smelled of turned soil, damp moss, and the faint tang of something herbal.

"Do you even know where you're going?" Evie hissed toward the cat.

Persephone didn't dignify her with a glance.

The moon pushed through a gap in the clouds just enough to make out the flattened grass ahead.

Footprints. Fresh.

Annabel leaned forward, peering into the dim. "There. The path splits just beyond the willows."

They rounded the bend—only to stop short.

Because someone was already there.

***

A figure in a long coat, crouched at the base of a hedgerow, gloved hands gently plucking what looked like... wild chamomile?

"Evening," said Ivy Gresham, not looking up. "Bit late for a riverside stroll, isn't it?"

Annabel blinked. "I could say the same."

Ivy straightened slowly, slipping her small shears back into a canvas satchel. "I'm harvesting. Moonlight pulls oils to the surface. Makes the plants more potent."

Evie crossed her arms. "Moonlight and murder in one day. We're all making the most of it."

Ivy tilted her head. "You're looking for someone."

"We're looking for Graham Forsyth," Annabel said, watching Ivy's face. "He slipped out of the Hare & Hound without a goodbye."

"And you think he's out here?"

Persephone meowed in affirmation, brushing past Ivy's boots without breaking stride.

"I saw someone pass this way about ten minutes ago," Ivy admitted, after a pause. "Quick steps. Dark coat. Looked... jittery."

Annabel raised a brow. "You didn't think to mention it?"

"I don't report every man pacing like a guilt-ridden squirrel," Ivy said dryly. "But since you're on the scent... he went left, down the slope. Toward the old boathouse."

Evie narrowed her eyes. "That's where the maintenance shed is, isn't it?"

"And the fishing platform," Annabel added.

Ivy's gaze flicked briefly down the path. "You'd better move quickly."

She turned to go, then paused.

"Annabel?"

"Yes?"

"If you find Graham... ask him what happened *three summers ago.*"

Annabel's brows pulled together. "Three summers ago?" she repeated. "That's a little cryptic, even for you."

Ivy shrugged, but her eyes said more than her tone. "It was quiet. Until it wasn't."

Evie stepped in. "What kind of 'not quiet' are we talking? A fistfight? A scandal? A cover-up involving someone's prize goose?"

Ivy hesitated.

"Let's just say," she said slowly, "Graham disappeared back then too. Only that time, he wasn't the only one."

Annabel blinked. "Someone else disappeared?"

"Not exactly," Ivy murmured. "But someone left. Quickly. And came back different."

"Who?"

Ivy just smiled, but there was no warmth in it.

"It's not my story to tell. But if you want to understand Graham... start there."

Evie was about to fire off another question, but Persephone let out an urgent chirp, tail high, already disappearing down the slope toward the river.

Annabel exhaled. "We'll talk again, Ivy."

"I'll be here," Ivy said. "Plants don't harvest themselves."

She vanished into the mist, the scent of chamomile trailing after her.

***

Annabel stared after her. "Three summers ago?"

Evie shook her head. "I swear, every villager has a timeline and a secret. You need a string board."

Persephone darted ahead with purpose, her tail twitching like punctuation.

Annabel followed.

***

Down by the river, the world narrowed — overgrown hedges, tangled roots, and the glimmer of water slipping past in silence. The old boathouse loomed in the near-dark — just a squat shape against the trees.

No light.

No sound.

Evie whispered, "You think he's in there?"

Annabel didn't answer.

She was already moving.

Chapter 6

The path to the old boathouse was little more than packed earth and memory.

As Annabel and Evie followed Persephone's flicking tail, the trees closed in slightly, the kind of darkness that felt not just *dim* but listening. River mist slid over the ground like breath.

"I don't like this," Evie muttered.

Annabel didn't respond. She was watching the shadows between the reeds. Listening for movement. The quiet was too complete.

The boathouse appeared at the edge of the clearing, slumped against the river like it had grown tired of standing.

One broken shutter flapped loosely.

***

They crept closer. Persephone stopped just shy of the door and sat.

Annabel whispered, "Do you smell anything?"

Evie sniffed. "Rot. Damp wood. And maybe... onions?"

Annabel pointed. "That's wild garlic."

Evie wrinkled her nose. "How rustic."

Annabel tested the door. Unlatched.

She looked at Evie.

"Let me guess," Evie whispered. "You're going in first?" Annabel pushed it open without a word.

***

The boathouse interior was a box of shadows.

Dust hung in the air. Old fishing gear, a cracked oar, and what looked like a mummified boot lined the walls. There was a narrow wooden bench along one side, and a table covered in a stiff, yellowing cloth.

But no Graham.

"He was supposed to be here," Annabel said softly.

Evie moved to the table, peeled back the cloth—revealing a notebook.

Worn. Leather. Buckled shut with an old ribbon. On the cover, in faded ink: "*A.F.*"

Annabel's breath caught. "Alistair Forsyth."

Evie opened it slowly.

Inside: neat, looping handwriting. Medical notes. Lists of symptoms. Pages of treatment plans.

But near the middle — a different kind of entry.

"*Three summers ago — Graham furious. Henry R. refused settlement. Margaret suggested we shred files. Told her no. I won't lie for him again.*"

Annabel and Evie exchanged a look.

Henry R. — Radcliffe.

Graham. Margaret. A settlement?

Annabel closed the book gently.

"We need to leave."

Evie blinked. "You're not going to say we should *take it?*"

Annabel shook her head. "Not yet. Let's make sure we weren't *followed* first."

Persephone hissed softly.

From outside... a crunch.

Of footsteps.

***

Annabel moved to the door and opened it slowly.

No one.

Evie looked around, nerves jangling. "Was that—?"

Annabel nodded. "Someone was watching us."

Persephone, still by the table, now pawed at the floor beneath it.

Annabel knelt, lifted the edge of a broken board — and revealed a small, sealed envelope, aged and brittle.

Inside: a photograph.

Graham and Alistair, standing outside the clinic. Smiling.

Behind them: a woman Annabel didn't recognize.

On the back:

"*Belladonna thrives in shade.*"

***

They left the boathouse with the envelope, the photo, and a thousand new questions.

Persephone led the way, her black tail cutting through the mist like a blade.

Evie exhaled. "So, who is the woman?"

Annabel looked at the photo again.

"I don't know."

But I think she's why someone's killing to bury the past.

Chapter 7

The photo sat on the kitchen table at Honeystone Cottage like a guest who wouldn't explain why she was here.

Annabel, tea in hand, stared at the faded image: Dr. Alistair Forsyth, Graham, and the unknown woman standing just behind them — smiling, slightly out of focus. Her hand rested lightly on Graham's arm, and the look she gave Alistair was... not friendly.

Evie, perched across the table with her boots on a stool, chewed on the end of a pencil. "The handwriting. 'Belladonna thrives in shade.' That's not a label. That's a *warning.*"

Annabel nodded slowly. "Or a confession."

Persephone flicked her tail once, the universal sign for *finally, they're catching on.*

***

They started where every village mystery should: Florence Cattermole, the WI's iron-fisted historian and tea tyrant, currently gardening beside her Victorian climbing clematis and pretending she hadn't been waiting for visitors all day.

Florence spotted the envelope in Annabel's hand before a single word was spoken.

"I haven't seen that picture in years," she said flatly.

Evie blinked. "You've *seen* it?"

Florence straightened. "Alistair had it on his desk. Tucked behind his calendar. That was... *before it all went wrong.*"

Annabel stepped forward. "Who is she?"

A pause. Then:

"Beatrice Hargreaves."

Evie frowned. "Any relation to—"

"Graham's ex. She used to work at the surgery. Temporary admin. Bright. Ambitious. Didn't take well to being told to 'mind her place.'"

"What happened to her?"

Florence dusted off her gloves, lips tight. "She left. One day she was here, the next—vanished. I heard she went up north.

Some say she married a banker. Some say she didn't."

Annabel handed her the photo. "Does the belladonna reference mean anything to you?"

Florence hesitated. "She used to say that. Whenever someone underestimated her. Said it was her 'personal proverb.'"

"*Belladonna thrives in shade. So do I.*"

***

Later, at the cottage, Evie was already halfway through a Google rabbit hole.

"Beatrice Hargreaves, no recent socials. No current address. But guess what?"

She turned the laptop to Annabel.

"There was a Beatrice Hargreaves listed as a witness in a medical ethics hearing. Three summers ago. In Leeds."

Annabel felt the air shift. "Alistair was involved?"

Evie nodded. "As a *silent advisor* on a clinic board. Her testimony? Sealed."

Persephone stretched luxuriously and knocked the photo off the table.

*****

Annabel stood, already grabbing her coat.

"Time to pay Dr. Graves a visit," she said.

Evie smirked. "Shall I bring snacks?"

Annabel checked her bag. "Bring gloves. Just in case he's growing something poisonous."

Persephone jumped up with a chirp and trotted to the door like, *finally.*

Chapter 8

Dr. Richard Graves's office was pristine. Annabel noted the arrangement immediately — books alphabetized *by author*, herbs in labelled jars, a single decorative houseplant that looked suspiciously fake.

The kind of space that said *I control everything*.

Graves stood to greet them. Crisp white shirt. Neutral smile. Hands folded like he was always ready for bad news.

"Miss Lennox Deighton. Miss Barnes. And of course... Persephone."

Persephone narrowed her eyes and sat directly in the centre of the rug, staring up at him like she'd already read his soul and found it... untidy.

***

"Thank you for seeing us," Annabel said smoothly. "We won't take much of your time."

"Of course. I'm always happy to help. Though I must admit," he added with a faint smile, "this seems more like a police matter now."

Evie raised an eyebrow. "And yet you weren't at the fair."

Graves folded his hands. "I've only recently arrived. I felt it best not to insert myself into village activities too quickly."

Annabel tilted her head. "Or perhaps you didn't want to insert yourself before the investigation concluded?"

A flicker of something — just a flash — passed through his eyes.

"I'm not sure I follow."

***

Annabel reached into her bag and placed the photo on the desk.

Alistair. Graham. Beatrice Hargreaves.

Graves didn't react — not with his face. But his fingers twitched once.

"Do you recognize her?" Annabel asked softly.

Graves exhaled. "That was... not part of my role."

Evie leaned in. "What *is* your role exactly?"

He didn't answer.

Persephone stood. Walked to the desk.

Annabel watched her, calmly, as the cat strolled behind Graves's polished chair... stopped at the small side table, and lifted one paw.

A clean, deliberate swipe.

A folder — thick, stamped with a faded "CONFIDENTIAL" seal — slid out from the bottom shelf.

It hit the floor with a soft thud.

Everyone stared at it.

Even Graves.

He didn't move.

Annabel stood, crossed the room, and picked it up.

Evie whistled low. "Oops."

***

Graves sat back down.

"I was sent by the board," he said, finally.

"They received multiple complaints over the past three years. About mistreatment. Negligence. Improper disposal of records. One case involved a... misdiagnosis that resulted in permanent injury. Another hinted at coercion. One included your friend, Miss Coombes."

Annabel's jaw tightened. "Margaret?"

"She never formally filed. But she was named… as a witness. Then retracted."

Annabel's voice was sharp. "So instead of a proper investigation, they sent you to poke around quietly?"

Graves looked tired now. "I wasn't meant to confront him. I was meant to observe. To collect. And when the board had enough… they would act."

Evie snapped, "And now he's dead."

Graves nodded slowly. "Yes."

***

Persephone hopped onto the desk like a furry mic drop.

Graves watched her with new respect. Or fear. Possibly both.

"I want that folder," Annabel said. "We'll return it. Eventually."

Graves didn't argue.

***

Outside, the wind had picked up.

Annabel tucked the folder into her coat. "He was hiding a lot."

Evie sighed. "And now we're the ones carrying it."

Persephone trotted ahead, tail high, ears perked — as if she knew the path only got darker from here.

Chapter 9

Back at Honeystone Cottage, the kettle had boiled. The curtains were drawn. Persephone was curled on the windowsill like a velvet punctuation mark.

But the room felt... colder.

Annabel and Evie sat at the table, the thick folder open between them — pages splayed out like fallen leaves, every one of them marked with quiet tragedy.

***

"Three complaints from 2019," Annabel read aloud. "One regarding a missed diagnosis of early-onset diabetes. One where he prescribed the wrong medication entirely. And this one—"

She paused.

Evie leaned in. "Go on."

"A seventeen-year-old girl... misdiagnosed. Sent home. Turned out to be meningitis. She died three days later."

Silence settled between them.

Evie broke it first. "How does a man like that stay in practice?"

Annabel shook her head. "There are excuses listed. Overwork. Staffing shortages. Notes from Graves suggesting that records were *lost*, not hidden. But this—" she tapped a page, voice hardening, "—this shows he altered notes after the fact."

Evie winced. "That's not a mistake. That's a cover-up."

***

Annabel flipped through more pages. "There's a pattern. Some of these patients never filed formal complaints. Others did... and suddenly retracted."

"Or the clinic 'lost the paperwork.'" Evie's voice dripped with disbelief.

They sat back, processing.

***

"The clinic staff must have known something," Annabel said finally.

"Margaret definitely would've. She was his right hand."

"Which means..." Annabel tapped the table, "either she helped protect him... or she was caught in it."

Evie bit her lip. "She's sharp. Observant. She'd notice if her doctor was making bad calls."

Annabel's voice was quiet now. "What if she wasn't just his nurse?"

Evie raised a brow. "You think there was something between them?"

"I think... she had *a reason* to stand by him. Whether it was love, loyalty, fear, or debt... I don't know yet."

Evie opened her mouth, then closed it again.

"Do we confront her?" she asked finally.

Annabel glanced toward the darkening window.

"Not yet."

***

She picked up a smaller slip of paper tucked between the reports. It was handwritten. Not official.

"I know I should've stopped him."
"But I didn't know where the line was anymore."

No signature. But Annabel was willing to bet it wasn't Alistair's handwriting.

***

Persephone leapt down and padded across the table, gently placing a paw on the unsigned note.

Evie blinked. "She's becoming unnervingly good at this."

Annabel smiled faintly, but her eyes stayed on the paper.

"We find out who wrote this. And then we ask Margaret why she let it happen."

Chapter 10

The lights were still on at the Little Firling Clinic, but just barely — one flickering lamp near the front desk, a muted glow from behind the frosted glass of the back office.

Annabel knocked lightly, then pushed the door open.

Sasha Eldridge sat behind the reception desk, hunched over a mug of tea and a half-eaten custard cream. Her blonde bob was slightly frizzy from the rain, and her expression was set to "I'm tired and one sigh away from a nervous breakdown."

When she saw Annabel, she didn't bother with a smile.

"Come to cancel your flu jab?"

Annabel stepped in slowly. "I was hoping to ask you something."

Sasha raised a brow. "I'm off the clock. But if it's not contagious, go ahead."

Annabel held out the folded note — the anonymous confession from Forsyth's file.

"Do you recognize the handwriting?"

Sasha stared at it for a beat too long. Then she blinked and looked away.

"Nope. Never seen it."

***

Persephone, who had slipped in behind Annabel like the *black silk ghost of truth*, jumped silently onto the reception desk and settled into a sphinx pose.

Sasha glared at her.

"That cat hates me."

Annabel smiled faintly. "She hates liars more."

Sasha scowled but didn't push her off the desk.

***

Annabel took a seat in one of the waiting room chairs. "You were here through most of Dr. Forsyth's career. You must have seen a lot."

Sasha stirred her tea with more aggression than necessary.

"I saw forms. I saw people yelling in the lobby. I saw Margaret crying in the stock cupboard. I saw Alistair pretending not to notice."

That caught Annabel's attention.

"Margaret cried?"

Sasha snorted. "Please. She was devoted to him. Worshipped the ground he walked on — and probably sprinkled antiseptic on it afterward."

"Was it personal?"

Sasha looked up. "He saved her once. Something happened... years ago. She never said what, but after that? She'd have taken a bullet for him."

Annabel considered that. "Or turned one into a syringe."

***

She placed the note gently on the desk again.

"If you didn't write this, who do you think did?"

Sasha hesitated. Then, with a shrug: "Could've been Graham. He used to sneak in here after hours. They fought. Once Alistair threw a clipboard at him. I heard it from the front. Next day, everything was quiet again."

"Why are you still here?" Annabel asked, softly now. "You've seen the files. You know what people are saying."

Sasha let out a long breath and stared into her tea like it held a map to another life.

"Because I don't know how to leave. This place is a mess, but it's *my* mess."

***

Persephone slowly stretched and flicked her tail into Sasha's tea saucer.

She hissed — not the cat. Sasha.

"Fine. Maybe I've seen that handwriting. Maybe once. On a post-it. Margaret leaves herself reminders in her locker. Stupid little mantras."

Annabel's eyes narrowed. "Mantras?"

Sasha shrugged. "'Do better,' 'don't speak,' 'remember why.' That kind of thing."

Evie, who had been leaning in the doorway the whole time, nodded. "Sounds like a woman trying to hold herself together with hope and denial."

Annabel paused, her hand on the note. "What about... other people? Patients.

Families. Did anyone ever come back angry?"

Sasha's eyes flicked to the clock on the wall, like she was debating how much more she wanted to say.

Then she sighed. "There was a woman. Mother of a girl who died — meningitis. Her name was Irene Holt. She came back a year later. Sat in the waiting room every Friday for a month. Said nothing. Just sat."

Evie frowned. "That's... chilling."

"She gave me a tin of biscuits," Sasha said, eyes distant. "Then one day she stopped coming."

Annabel narrowed her gaze. "What happened to her?"

"She lives just outside the village now. On the edge of Firling Cross. Walks with a cane. Her husband—" Sasha lowered her voice "—he blamed Alistair. Fully. Told me once that if karma didn't do the job, he might have to."

Evie made a low whistle. "Well, that's not ominous at *all.*"

Annabel leaned in. "Who else?"

"Bryn Lewis. Claimed Alistair prescribed him a drug cocktail that made his heart worse. Alistair swore it was patient error. Bryn swore it was medical arrogance."

Evie scribbled notes. "And is he the subtle revenge type?"

Sasha snorted. "He once superglued a rude note to the clinic door."

***

Annabel stood.

"Thank you."

Sasha gave a tight, wry smile. "If you tell anyone I was helpful, I'll deny it."

Persephone flicked her tail again — this time lightly tapping the edge of the confession note as if to say: *You're getting warmer.*

Chapter 11

The next morning brought mist and low clouds, the kind of sky that threatened rain but hadn't quite committed — perfect weather for secrets.

Annabel and Evie took the long way toward Firling Cross, passing hedgerows heavy with dew and daffodils bowing in silence.

Persephone, despite Annabel's suggestion that she stay warm inside, had simply stared at her, offended, and trotted after them with her usual purposeful grace.

"We're not accusing anyone yet," Annabel said, mostly to herself.

"We're observing," Evie replied. "Like passive-aggressive village wildlife experts."

The cottage of Irene Holt was small, set at the edge of a field lined with hawthorns. Neat lawn. Pristine rose beds. But the curtains stayed closed.

Annabel knocked. They waited. Then the door creaked open a fraction.

Irene Holt looked older than she should have — not in years, but in posture. Her eyes were sharp, her cardigan threadbare at the elbows.

"You're not selling anything, are you?"

Annabel shook her head gently. "We're asking about Dr. Forsyth."

A long pause.

Then: "Dead, is he?"

Evie blinked. "You didn't know?"

"I knew something had shifted. The village goes quieter when someone finally gets what they deserve."

Annabel hesitated. "Do you believe someone did this deliberately?"

Irene's expression didn't change. "I believe justice comes eventually. The method is irrelevant."

Persephone meowed softly.

Irene looked down. "That cat always did like my garden."

"You sat in the clinic lobby. Fridays."

"I did." She opened the door a little wider. "To remind him I hadn't forgotten. To make him look at what he'd done, every week."

"Why did you stop?"

"Because   eventually...   he   stopped looking back."

The door closed.

***

They found Bryn Lewis outside The Hare & Hound, smoking something that probably wasn't legal and aggressively sanding a walking stick.

"Thought you'd be sniffing around soon enough," he grunted.

Annabel nodded. "We heard you had a history with the doctor."

"History? That man put me on a drug that nearly killed me. Then blamed *me* for taking it wrong."

Evie raised an eyebrow. "You seem pretty alive."

"Oh, I'm alive. *He's not.* Convenient, innit?"

Annabel studied him. "Did you ever tell him you'd get revenge?"

Bryn looked up sharply. "I *told everyone.* If karma didn't take him, I'd finish the job."

Evie leaned in. "So... karma's timing saved you the effort?"

He didn't flinch. "Maybe."

Annabel took a step closer. "And now?"

He exhaled. "Now I get to fix up me shed in peace. And no one's knocking asking for bloody wellness brochures."

"But you didn't do it," Annabel said softly.

"Didn't say I didn't," he shot back —
and walked away, whistling.

***

Later, back at the cottage, Evie flopped
into a chair. "So, Irene's intense and poetic.
Bryn's just... mad."

Annabel flipped through the file again.

"Both had motive. But neither had
access. Neither knew about the internal
review. Neither had tea with him on the
day."

Evie nodded slowly. "We've circled the
garden beds. And all the footprints lead
back..."

"To the surgery," Annabel said. "And to
Margaret."

Persephone gave a single, pointed chirp.

"Alright, alright," Evie muttered. "Time to repot some secrets."

Chapter 12

The garden behind Margaret Coombes' cottage was immaculate.

Box hedges trimmed to within an inch of their lives. Lavender pruned to perfect symmetry. Not a single weed dared peek through the gravel path. If control were a place, this would be it.

Annabel, with Evie beside her and Persephone at her heels, knocked once on the back gate.

It opened before she could knock again.

Margaret stood in her gardening gloves, a smear of compost on her cheek, eyes wary.

"If you're here for gossip, I suggest the pub."

Annabel held up the manila folder — Forsyth's internal review — and the folded note with Margaret's unmistakable handwriting.

"We're here for the truth."

***

Inside, the kettle was already hissing, as if Margaret had been expecting them.

She poured the tea with calm hands but tight lips. The mugs were plain. The tension was not.

"You've read the file," she said, more statement than question.

Annabel nodded. "We know there were complaints. Patterns. A system built to hide failure."

Evie added, "And someone who tried —
quietly — to stop it."

She slid the note forward.

I know I should've stopped him.

*But I didn't know where the line was
anymore.*

Margaret stared at it.

She didn't deny it.

***

"He saved my life," she said quietly,
finally. "Years ago. A cancer scare. He
caught it early. Pushed for tests when no
one else believed me. I survived because of
him."

A long breath.

"So, when the complaints started… I didn't want to believe them. I thought — people make mistakes. He was overworked. Tired. Maybe they were wrong."

Annabel said nothing.

"But then Graham came back. Angry. Vicious. Dragging up the past. And I saw… *Alistair change.* He started second-guessing himself. Then blaming others. Then… hiding things."

Evie's voice was gentle. "Why didn't you report him?"

"Because I loved him," Margaret whispered. "Not romantically. Not even as a friend. But with that kind of *terrible, desperate loyalty* that makes you blind."

Persephone jumped onto the kitchen counter and knocked over a small ceramic pot.

Inside? A torn scrap of paper.

Margaret flinched.

Annabel retrieved it. A page from a diary?

"Graham won't stop. Beatrice was just the beginning. He'll ruin everything."

Evie's eyes widened. "So, there was something with Beatrice."

Margaret nodded, tears now slipping down her cheek silently.

"They had a relationship. Quiet. Complicated. She left after something went wrong. I never knew the whole story, only that Graham blamed Alistair. And when she was called to testify... Alistair *panicked*."

Annabel leaned in. "Did Graham kill him?"

Margaret shook her head.

"I don't know. But I know Graham *wanted to confront him at the fair.* He said... he had something that would end it all."

"And you?" Annabel asked softly. "Did you have something to protect?"

Margaret looked up, broken but unashamed.

"Only what I believed in. Until it shattered."

***

They left in silence.

Persephone paused at the gate, tail flicking once.

Evie murmured, "She's not guilty. But she's not innocent either."

Annabel looked toward the village green.

"Then we'd better find the person who is."

Chapter 13

The Firling Downs Racetrack wasn't glamorous. It smelled of stale ale, damp turf, and fried onions — and the punters ranged from weathered pros in tweed caps to locals squinting at racing slips like they were trying to decode ancient runes.

Annabel, Evie, and Persephone (smuggled in via determined handbag) made their way through the small Saturday crowd toward the food stall near the paddock — where a familiar hunched figure was slumped over a polystyrene tray of chips and gravy.

Graham Forsyth.

***

He looked up before they spoke.

"I figured you'd find me."

Annabel sat beside him on the low brick ledge. "We've got questions."

"I'm not surprised." He took a chip. "You want to know if I killed my brother."

Evie said, "We want to know what you're not telling us."

***

Graham stared out at the track for a long moment.

"I left the village on Friday afternoon," he said. "Took the train. Stayed overnight in Mickleham with an old mate — Freddy Lowes. He's got CCTV on his front porch, and a timestamped pizza delivery at 8:12 p.m."

Annabel raised an eyebrow. "And the next morning?"

"We didn't leave the house until ten. Watched the early races from his sofa. I've got time-stamped betting receipts from the app. You want them?"

Evie nodded slowly. "So, you couldn't have tampered with the tea."

"Didn't touch his mug, his herbs, his bloody flower collection. Last time I saw Alistair, it was three weeks ago. And yes, we shouted. I wanted him to come clean. But I didn't kill him."

***

Annabel held out the photo.

"Tell me about Beatrice."

Graham flinched.

"He ruined her," he said quietly. "He gaslit her, made her think she was paranoid. She caught him shredding test results. She confronted him."

"What happened?"

"He called her unstable. Got her transferred. Then blackballed her from three clinics."

Evie frowned. "But she testified against him?"

Graham nodded.

"She used a different name. Bea Holloway. After her mother's maiden name. She told the board *everything.* But it was sealed. Quiet settlement. She went off the radar."

Annabel's eyes sharpened. "Until now?"

Graham nodded. "She reached out. Said she was thinking of coming back. She wanted closure. Said she might even talk to a reporter."

"Did Alistair know?"

"I think he *suspected.* He was on edge. Cleaning up files. Panicking."

***

Annabel sat back.

"Do you think someone killed him to protect him?"

Graham laughed — bitter and cracked. "No one ever protected Alistair. Not really.

People just let him lie. And sometimes that's worse."

***

They left Graham staring out at the track.

Persephone trotted beside them, silent, thoughtful.

Evie spoke first. "So... he's not our killer."

Annabel sighed. "No. But he might have gotten someone else killed."

Evie blinked. "Beatrice?"

Annabel nodded. "If she was coming back... someone might've wanted to stop her too."

Chapter 14

The clinic was closed for the afternoon. A printed sign on the door read "Staff Training," but Annabel and Evie both knew that was code for Dr. Graves Wants Everyone Gone.

Which made it the perfect time to knock.

Persephone, naturally, slinked in before the door had fully opened.

Dr. Graves didn't look surprised to see them.

"I wondered when you'd come back."

Annabel walked in calmly. "We need more."

He gestured to the chairs across from his desk. The room still smelled faintly of mint and antiseptic — too clean for real peace.

***

"We've identified Beatrice," Annabel began. "She's using the name Bea Holloway. We know she testified. You had to know that too."

Graves folded his hands. "Her name was redacted in the version you saw. I had the full file."

Evie narrowed her eyes. "And you didn't think to tell us?"

"It wasn't relevant to the board investigation anymore. She disappeared after the hearing. No forwarding contact. No one's seen her in nearly two years."

Annabel leaned in. "Did you look?"

Graves blinked. "No."

"Then you underestimated her. She was planning to return."

That caught him off guard. His posture shifted slightly. "How do you know?"

Evie grinned. "Oh, you know. The way women do — via breadcrumbs, cats, and furious ex-boyfriends."

***

Annabel shifted the tone.

"We want to talk about Alistair's wife. Delia Forsyth. Died two years ago. Reported as natural causes. No autopsy."

A long silence.

"She'd been sick," Graves said finally. "Autoimmune complications."

"Did she trust him?" Annabel asked.

Graves didn't answer.

Evie: "Did *you* trust him?"

Graves hesitated — then stood. Moved to the bookshelf.

From behind a row of journals, he pulled out a sealed envelope, unmarked, thick.

He laid it on the desk.

"This... didn't go in the board report. It was left anonymously in my clinic box a month ago. No name. Just a note that read: '*He's done it before.*'"

Annabel opened the envelope.

Inside were a copy of Delia Forsyth's prescription history, her patient notes (some with worrying gaps) and a note in shaky handwriting: *She didn't want the pills. She stopped taking them. But he kept pushing.*

***

Evie whispered, "Do you think he poisoned her?"

Graves said nothing. But he didn't deny it.

***

"And who else?" Annabel pressed. "You've seen the files. Talked to staff. Who else hated him?"

Graves sat again. "Not everyone hated him. Some feared him. Some depended on him. But..."

He pulled out another paper.

"There was a complaint from a former staff member. A name you might recognize. Maggie Cooke."

Annabel looked up sharply. "The baker?"

"She was," Graves said. "These days she runs the flower shop. Said she needed something quieter."

He paused. "People find their own way to heal, I suppose."

"Used to be a care assistant. Worked with Alistair when he did elder home visits. Filed a concern... then retracted it."

Annabel leaned back. "Why retract it?"

Graves folded the papers away. "He had a way of making people feel small. Stupid. Overreactive. Especially women."

Annabel's voice went quiet. "So, this whole village was trained to excuse him."

Persephone jumped onto the desk, stared Graves down, and gave a low growl.

***

Outside, the clouds were gathering.

Inside, the storm had already begun.

Chapter 15

The scent hit them before the bell did — a heady swirl of lilies, eucalyptus, and something faintly citrus that Evie immediately suspected was "a soap trying too hard."

The window read:

Cooke & Vine – Flowers for Every Season

...in curling gold script Annabel was pretty sure Florence Cattermole hated.

As they stepped inside, Evie muttered, "Last year she was frosting cupcakes and threatening anyone who said her almond tarts were dry."

Annabel smiled. "She was in a coma, Evie. Some people take up journaling. Maggie took up floristry."

Evie shrugged. "Trauma and begonias. Could be worse."

*****

Inside, Maggie Cooke was elbow-deep in white roses and dusty miller, tying ribbons with a focus that could've defused a bomb. The shop was warm, filled with soft jazz and barely controlled chaos — glass vases clinked faintly, and someone had overwatered the ferns again.

"If you're here for last-minute peonies in March," Maggie said without looking up, "save us all the drama."

Annabel stepped forward. "Not flowers. Just truth."

***

Maggie didn't flinch, but the ribbon in her hand tore.

She straightened slowly, brushing off her apron, eyes landing briefly on Persephone, who had jumped onto the counter and was eyeing a duck-shaped ceramic planter like it owed her money.

"I figured someone would come knocking."

Evie glanced around. "Didn't think it'd be in a flower shop, to be honest. You used to bake."

Maggie gave a tired smirk. "Flour started giving me flashbacks."

Annabel's voice was gentle. "So, you changed course."

"Yeah," Maggie said. "Baking felt loud. Flowers don't scream when things go wrong."

***

Annabel laid the note on the counter.

The shaky handwriting. The weight of implication.

She didn't want the pills. She stopped taking them. But he kept pushing.

"You've seen this before," Annabel said. "Haven't you?"

Maggie nodded.

"Pinned to the back of Delia's medicine cabinet. I found it during a home visit. Didn't think anyone else had noticed."

"You filed a complaint," Annabel said. "Then you retracted it."

"Because the next day, my mum — who needed a prescription urgently — suddenly ended up at the bottom of the patient list. Deliberate or not, Margaret delivered the message with a smile and a 'maybe you misunderstood.'"

Evie winced. "That's calculated."

Maggie looked down. "It was protection. She thought she was keeping everything afloat. Or maybe just keeping *him* afloat."

***

"Did you know Bea Holloway?" Annabel asked.

Maggie flinched, just slightly. "Everyone knew Bea. Smart. Brave. Too good for the place."

"She left?"

"She ran. After she found something. I never knew what — just that it shook her. She said, 'They buried Delia. They'll bury this too.' Then she vanished."

Evie leaned in. "But she told you she was going to the board?"

"Yes. Then I never heard from her again."

***

Persephone chose that moment to knock the duck planter off the counter.

It hit the floor. Shattered.

Maggie didn't flinch.

Evie muttered, "She's so dramatic lately."

Annabel, still watching Maggie, said softly, "And who else might have known what Bea found?"

Maggie took a breath. "Maybe Colin Denby. He used to garden for the Forsyths. He was quiet, but he saw things."

"Like what?"

"Like Delia talking to the birds. Or crying in the rose beds. Like how her prescriptions changed, even when she didn't."

Annabel nodded slowly. "Colin it is, then."

***

They left without another word.

As the door shut behind them, Evie said, "So, Maggie's not a killer."

Annabel looked ahead, thoughtful. "No. But she saw the roots. She just couldn't stop the bloom."

Persephone flicked her tail once — like a full stop on a sentence no one wanted to finish.

Chapter 16

Colin Denby's cottage sat at the far edge of Little Firling, hidden behind a thicket of old hazels and flowering quince. The kind of place most villagers forgot existed — which was exactly how Colin liked it.

Annabel, Evie, and Persephone followed the worn path to his crooked gate, where a carved wooden sign read: "Tread Softly — Roots Remember."

Evie muttered, "That's not creepy at all."

***

Colin answered the door in mud-stained trousers and a jumper that had known better decades. His hair, like the moss on his fence, was unbothered by time or trimming.

"Ladies," he said, blinking slowly. "And Miss Persephone."

The cat, of course, walked in first.

***

His home smelled of dried thyme, old books, and peat. The living room had more plants than chairs. A teapot steamed quietly beside a half-finished puzzle of some ancient ruin overtaken by ivy.

"What brings you to my overgrown corner?" he asked, pouring tea into mismatched mugs.

Annabel held up the photo — Alistair, Graham, and Bea.

"We know she used the name Bea Holloway. We think you knew her."

Colin looked down at the photo, then at Persephone.

"She used to sit right there," he said, pointing to the windowsill. "Said the light made her feel honest."

Evie asked softly, "Did she write to you?"

Colin didn't answer. But Persephone jumped onto a nearby shelf and began batting at a row of old gardening journals.

Thump. One fell to the floor.

Inside: a letter.

***

Annabel opened it.

Handwritten. Folded twice. Dated two weeks before the fair.

Colin,

I've decided. I'm coming back. I can't let him die thinking he won. If I vanish again, let them know I tried.

— Bea

Annabel's voice was steady. "You didn't tell anyone?"

Colin's hands trembled slightly. "She trusted me. Said she needed a week to gather evidence. I didn't want to betray that."

Evie frowned. "Did you tell Alistair she was coming?"

"No. But I think Margaret knew. Somehow. She always knew things she shouldn't."

***

Annabel looked at the letter again. "Why was she so afraid?"

Colin stared into his tea.

"Because she knew what happened to Delia. And she knew Alistair wasn't done hiding things."

A long silence.

"I was supposed to meet her. The morning after the fair. She never showed."

✳✳✳

Outside, the wind picked up.

Inside, Persephone curled beside the cold hearth, eyes half-lidded — like she'd just solved the case and was waiting for everyone else to catch up.

Chapter 17

The Hare & Hound was quieter than usual, but no less nosy.

The bunting from the garden fair still sagged in the corner, a few stray petals scattered on the hearth. A fire burned low, and the gossip burned higher.

Annabel and Evie slid into their usual booth with a quiet nod from Henry Griggs, the bartender, who poured their drinks without asking.

Persephone leapt up beside them, ignored the sardine pâté this time, and instead perched like an interrogator waiting for the next suspect.

"You can feel it," Evie murmured. "Everyone's jumpy."

Annabel nodded. "We just have to let them talk."

TABLE ONE: Florence Cattermole, sharp as ever

"You ask me, Margaret's barely left the house since the fair. Keeps her curtains closed all day. Which is suspicious, *unless she's got something hideous blooming in her garden.*"

Evie whispered, "Or a conscience."

***

TABLE TWO: Sasha Eldridge, hunched over her cider

Sasha sat alone, flipping a beer mat, her knee bouncing.

Henry approached her with a drink. She looked up.

"Thanks," she muttered. "Even though I'm off the rota."

He gave a small smile. "Clinic's not the same without your whispering rage."

Sasha huffed. "It's not rage. It's repressed trauma and caffeine withdrawal."

She paused.

Then added quietly, "You know, he used to mix up prescriptions when Margaret was off. I always corrected them. But if I hadn't... I wonder how many people would've been hurt."

Annabel and Evie shared a look.

"Did you ever report it?" Evie asked.

Sasha glanced around. "No. Because Margaret would say I was overreacting. And she *ran* that place. Not Alistair. Not even the board. It was *her* clinic."

***

TABLE THREE: Colin, surprisingly talkative now

He waved them over with a glass of ginger wine.

"I remembered something," he said softly. "Day of the fair. I saw Margaret early — before it opened. She was headed toward the green, carrying something in a thermos flask."

Annabel blinked. "A thermos?"

"She said it was special tonic. For the 'guest tent.' But she walked past the tent entirely."

Evie leaned in. "Where did she go?"

"Toward the tea stall."

***

Silence. Weighty. Confirming.

Persephone gave a long, slow blink.

***

As they left, Evie whispered, "Sasha corrects Alistair's mistakes, Margaret overrules the staff, and Colin saw her with *the flask*."

Annabel's jaw tightened. "She didn't just know what Alistair did."

"She tried to stop it being exposed."

Persephone meowed.

“She *killed* to protect a lie.”

Chapter 18

The garden behind Margaret Coombes' cottage was still too perfect.

Even the wind couldn't muss the hedges. The lavender stood like soldiers. But today, the flowers didn't comfort — they stared.

Annabel rang the bell.

Evie crossed her arms.

Persephone curled on the stone wall, unblinking.

Margaret opened the door wearing her usual cardigan, her hair pulled into a neat twist. But her eyes looked tired — like she'd been up all-night waiting for this exact moment.

"Come to accuse me, then?"

Annabel didn't blink. "We came for the truth."

Margaret stepped aside.

***

Inside, tea was already steeping.

"Chamomile?" Margaret offered.

Evie looked at the mug like it was ticking. "Hard pass."

They sat at the small table. Margaret took her cup but didn't sip.

***

Annabel placed a folder on the table.

"Sasha told us about the prescription errors. About how you made the clinic run. Not Alistair."

Margaret said nothing.

"Colin saw you the morning of the fair. With a thermos."

Still nothing.

"You told him it was for the guest tent. But you never went there. You went to the tea stall."

Margaret set her cup down. The tiniest tremble in her hand.

Evie leaned forward. "Was it poison? Or medicine he didn't need?"

Margaret closed her eyes.

"It was belladonna."

Silence.

Even the kettle on the hob seemed to pause.

***

"He wasn't supposed to die," Margaret said finally, voice cracked open. "Just sleep through the fair. Miss his speech. Delay the scandal."

Annabel's voice was low. "You wanted to protect him."

"I wanted to protect the *idea* of him," Margaret whispered. "The doctor who saved me. The man who fought the board. Who held it together while everything around him rotted."

She opened her eyes.

"But he changed. After Delia. After Bea. He started silencing everything that threatened him. And when I found out Bea was coming back..."

Annabel finished it for her. "You panicked."

Margaret nodded. "He said he'd handle it. And I believed him. Until I saw the envelope she sent — unopened, in his bin. He never planned to listen. He was going to bury her. Again."

***

Evie spoke. "So, you brewed the tea."

"I put in just enough belladonna to make him groggy. Nothing fatal. I swear it."

Annabel stared at her. "But it was."

Margaret swallowed. "He had a heart condition. One I didn't know about. It... accelerated everything."

"You were his nurse," Evie said. "You should have known."

Margaret looked at her, eyes shining.

"I stopped being his nurse a long time ago. I was just the shadow holding his secrets."

***

Outside, a robin chirped like it didn't know the world had changed.

Persephone hopped off the wall and scratched once at the door. Then sat. Waiting.

"Will you turn me in?" Margaret asked.

Annabel stood.

"You already did."

Margaret's hands were clenched in her lap now, the tea untouched.

"He ruined everything he touched. Not all at once — in small ways. Quiet ones."

Annabel asked softly, "Is that what happened with Bea?"

Margaret nodded. "She wanted to believe the system would work. That the board would listen. But when they didn't... she fell apart. The only person who kept her grounded was Ivy."

Annabel blinked. "Ivy Gresham?"

"They were close. Ivy's the one who told her to leave. Said she'd water her garden until she was strong enough to come back."

Evie narrowed her eyes. "Did Ivy know what you planned?"

Margaret frowned. "No. I never told her."

Annabel went still.

So did Persephone.

A shadow moved outside in the garden of Margaret.

Chapter 19

The sun was pale when they reached Ivy Gresham's cottage — a soft gold filtered through the last of spring's clouds.

Her garden was blooming in quiet chaos.

Yarrow, sage, valerian, feverfew. Things with lovely names and darker uses.

Annabel, Evie, and Persephone stood at the gate.

Ivy was already in the herb beds, snipping something into a wide straw basket.

"Hello," she said without turning. "I thought you'd come."

***

They walked slowly through the rows. The air smelled like lemon balm and wet earth.

Persephone padded along the path, then stopped abruptly — her gaze fixed on a patch of tall green stalks near the back fence.

Foxglove.

Purple. Heavy-headed. Blooming strong.

Annabel stopped beside her. "That's unusual for your garden."

Ivy didn't look up. "Not really. It thrives in shade."

***

Evie's voice was quiet. "Margaret says you were close to Bea."

"I still am. We write."

Annabel stepped forward. "You knew she was coming back."

Ivy clipped a sprig of wormwood. "She'd made up her mind."

"So why didn't you let her finish it?"

That was when Ivy looked up.

Her face was calm. Not guilty. Not defensive. Just... still. "Because she didn't need to."

***

"You slipped the foxglove into the tea," Annabel said.

"I did."

"Why?"

Ivy rose slowly, wiping her hands on her apron.

"Because Margaret's plan wouldn't work. Alistair wouldn't sleep. He'd adapt. He'd spin. He'd crush Bea again, just like before. And she would break all over again."

Evie's voice was hoarse. "So, you killed him for her?"

Ivy looked at them, the wind catching the hem of her dress, the foxglove swaying behind her.

"I killed him for what he'd already done. And for what he would've done again. I knew the dosage. I measured it precisely. It was clean. Quick. Quiet."

Annabel stepped closer. "Bea didn't know."

"Of course not. She's the truth-teller. I'm the weed-puller."

***

Persephone walked to Ivy's feet and sat; tail wrapped like a question mark.

Ivy looked down.

"I don't regret it," she said softly. "You can tell the police, if that's your next step."

Annabel didn't answer right away.

She looked at the foxglove. At the garden. At the woman who saved her friend in the most final way possible.

Then she said: "I think some things thrive in shade because they have no choice."

Epilogue

Spring had shifted to early summer, and Honeystone Cottage was fully awake now — the New Dawn climbing rose halfway up the trellis, Desdemona glowing by the kitchen door, and Double Delight opening like it had just remembered it was the most beautiful thing in the garden.

Annabel knelt in the herb bed, gently tucking a sprig of bronze fennel beside the lemongrass.

"You're dramatic," she murmured to it. "You'll get along with the cat."

Persephone, as if summoned, stretched on the windowsill with theatrical flair and then blinked at a bee like it was beneath her.

Inside, the kettle was on. Evie was at the table, flipping through the latest issue of *British Gardening for the Slightly Suspicious.*

"So, Margaret's moved to Devon. Retirement by exile?"

Annabel nodded. "She said she wanted to grow sweet peas and not talk to anyone for three years. Reasonable."

"And Bea?"

Annabel smiled. "Bea's staying in the Cotswolds for now. Writing again. Ivy sends her dried herbs in unlabelled brown packets and handwritten notes that could be either recipes or coded warnings."

Evie chuckled. "Therapeutic."

"Potentially criminal," Annabel said, pouring tea. "But very therapeutic."

***

She settled into her chair and glanced toward the window, where the sun was hitting the foxglove just behind the low stone wall.

Yes, she'd planted one.

Just one.

And only in deep shade.

Evie raised an eyebrow at her. "You know, you didn't quote a single author the entire time."

Annabel blinked. "Did I not?"

Persephone gave her a judging look.

Annabel sipped her tea.

"Very well, if it must be remedied... *In time, we hate that which we often fear.*"

Evie smirked. "Shakespeare?"

Annabel nodded. "Troilus and Cressida."

"Very brooding of you."

"I'm in my tragic heroine arc. Let me have it."

***

The church bell rang once. Someone trimmed a hedge too enthusiastically down the lane. Somewhere, bees kept working like nothing had happened.

And in the centre of it all, Persephone blinked slowly — as if to say: *until next time.*

Murder Beneath the Ballroom Chandelier

A Little Firling Mystery – Book Three

An elegant gala. A vanished heirloom. A duchess who drops dead before dessert.

When Annabel Lennox Deighton is invited to Everly House for an opulent heritage ball, she expects roses, champagne, and mild gossip.

She does not expect murder under a chandelier.

But in Little Firling, nothing stays polished for long...